Whispers
from the Cave

Florencio Guevara

ISBN
978-1-954168-03-9 (Paperback)
978-1-954168-02-2 (eBook)

DEDICATION . . .

This book, like all my projects, is dedicated to the person
who is everything in life...my wife, Elvia, with love.....

TABLE OF CONTENTS

TABLE OF CONTENTS

A CAVE OF YOUR OWN

Words evolve in definition over the centuries as well as from one path in life to another. The word "cave" is a case in point. For mediums the word originates as "boveda"—[BO-vay-dah]. The boveda consists of a grouping of glass goblets representing the spiritual quadrant of each medium. Boveda can also mean hidden treasure box. Indeed this spiritual cave is a sanctuary from which our entities whisper their messages to us.

Your boveda can take shape in a number of ways. Some follow traditional formats, while others are less bound to doctrine. There are a large number of mediums who use seven glasses. This arrangement is usually one glass, flanked by six others. The center cave will usually hold a crucifix, with its lower half in the water, and facing the person. Seven being an obvious number of mystery, this tradition is probably the most in use. It also is associated with the African religion of the Yoruba, known as Santeria.

Another tradition for the boveda is the use of nine glasses. Nine is the universal number of the spirit or "muerto". Mediums who are very involved in passing their quadrants, as well as holding and sending spirits without light up to the "spiritual colleges, will more likely use this number of glasses. The number nine itself will attract entities with ease.

Still another shape for your boveda is the use of three glasses. These should be arranged for past, present, and future scrying, seeing in the waters…. The crucifix with this arrangement is usually a standing one, or it's laying down on the table.

It's important to note that the boveda can also have your own personal stamp on it. It all depends on what your spirits are inspiring you to do. I've seen some very fancy bovedas where the goblets have specific designs, such as Chinese calligraphy, African symbols, or ribbons of different colors tied around the lip of the goblet, or down by the stem.

Still others have goblets made of wood, or stained glass. Mediums come in all sizes, shapes, and styles. I know a few who have to invest in wall-to-wall tables. They will have a glass or goblet for each and every spirit they can identify in their Spirit Quadrant. Twenty plus glasses are almost normal for these mediums.

Each medium must work according the his/her Quadrant's directive. The inspiration that the spirit guides bestow upon the medium will inspire the type of boveda that they will be comfortable with. Inclusive, as mediums develop through the years, they could change the makeup of the "caves" so that their growth is reflected.

Me? I'm a lover of simplicity. Simplicity with beauty and direct attraction for any who visit my boveda. I keep my glasses small, plain, surrounding a small goblet. Indeed, I always get a kick out of the look on people's faces when they realize how small my boveda is! I chuckle as I think to myself, size has nothing to do with putting it to use with skill….!

All of this talk of how many glasses should a boveda have, brings me to another raging argument among the mediums.

It's an argument that's been around all too long, and it's time to put it to rest, so the axe can be buried. This conversation has often degenerated into outright confrontation, even within matrimony.

One boveda. No, two! Are you kidding, there are too many people there, they need six! Just one for all with a glass for all.…

And so it goes, ranging from the logical to the ridiculous. Now think. Each person is a unique vibration within the universe. No two people vibrate the same. This means that the way each person spiritually "works" is an individual signature in the world, there are no copies—not even identical twins can claim each other's vibration. The very fact that they were separated by minutes, reflects the difference in their astrological birth charts.

No matter how many people are living together, as long as each has a Spiritual Quadrant and is a medium, a separate boveda for each is essential…! We can't have our spirits and our paths tossed together like a salad. The identity of every medium must always be preserved, and reflected, in their boveda. Each one of these caves (glasses) will whisper in the spirit ear on a plane of thought that only that particular medium will "read".

If we had to share cell phones, with each person's contact mixed together, our cell phones would soon go haywire, not to mention the headaches and arguments among the people using them. The boveda works the same way. Your spirits—and only your spirits—know how to communicate with you. Symbols, words, sounds, pictures, particular memories and many more differing signals will be sent to each medium. This is their way of understanding their own, particular Spirit Quadrant.

I think I've stressed the point of individual bovedas, and their importance in spiritual development.

Yet, there is one exception to all of these arrangements. Just as there are family altars, where the blood relatives are remembered with photos and candles or incense, there can be a family boveda.

If you are going to go this route, note that everyone in the home must agree to this. A central place must be chosen. A very large goblet must be chosen as the center piece. This cave's water will be to protect and attract the family's over-all guardians of the family's safety and health. Each person living in the house will then choose the type of goblet they wish to represent them and their Quadrant. Some can choose to put a specific color ribbon on the stem to identify whose cave it is. Others, still, can choose a particular color of glass or goblet. The size is also an individualized choice, as long as it is not larger than the main family goblet.

However, if there is a working medium in the home, who readily attends misas or conducts readings for the public, then they will need their own boveda, in addition to having a goblet representing them at the family cave. This will keep the family boveda from having to be changed so much because of collecting too many vibes from the outside.

I have seen some very beautiful family bovedas in my time. It is a place that can help you bury the day's stress away...

Just ponder this thought: your boveda is like a computer server that only communicates with your reception. Your body knows all too well what the magic vibrational pitch to your receptacle is...

SHORT CIRCUITS AND FLYING SPARKS

Teaching a medium to develop is one of the most satisfying endeavors in my life. Weathering the doubts and traumas of channeling spirits is a step in growth we all experience. Without the shadow of a doubt, this is the most difficult and dangerous of all the mediumnistic skills possible.

Many a godchild of mine has voiced fear of allowing another entity to use his/her senses to communicate or work with an individual client. I always answer them with this statement. I always feel some fear when channeling even my own spirits. Whoever says they don't is playing with the truth. Remember that channeling is putting yourself atop the "fence" between life and death!

This process should never be taken under a devil-may-care, nonchalant attitude. The gravity of the process couldn't be stronger. Eagerness to learn is the essential requirement of all godchildren. However, that eagerness should never be supplanted by an overly confident, flippant disposition toward communicating with the "dead".

One of the first things to do is sit in front of your boveda in a comfortable, solid chair. There are spirits that will shake, rattle, and roll you r spinal cord! A flimsy chair will never do.....

The first order of business, of course, is prayer. The Lord's Prayer, Hail Mary, and Glory Be to God are the cornerstone. Then come selected prayers and meditations that your elder should be teaching you, in order to develop your antenna. These could be selected from specific books that have long been used over the years and through their experience within the Great Work.

First, the thought communications emanating from a spirit will come in the way of picture frames in lightning speed. You "know" what this spirit is presenting to you. Your thoughts begin to interact and merge with these thought patterns. At this moment you will form a sentence in your mind that will either describe the scene in your head, or speaks to the actions of that scene, either in defense or against the scene being depicted.

In these few *seconds* the medium is expected to voice the spirit's desired communication!

Yes, people, *seconds*. In the meantime, just as this is taking place, the medium will feel the vibration of the spirit. Raised hairs, jolts to the area of the spine, and shivers are all normal reactions. Remember that when two force fields attract, there is a friction that occurs as these two bodies of different energy sources merge and—in seconds—have the moment reach the intended mode of the medium able to speak, act, and help the client.

To help both yourself and the spirit merge effectively, raise both your hands more or less near both ears. Palms should be facing the skull. Then, gently at first, in a circular, backward motion, begin moving your arms simultaneously. As you move your hands and arms in this circular, backward motion, you will feel the vibration increase. Your system may become more agitated, and heartbeat could accelerate noticeably. Think of this as "wrapping" yourself with the entity. As the moments pass, you must increase your speed of hand movement near the back of your head as fast as you can. Do not be surprised if you feel the speed pick up by itself. This is the spirit's vibration interacting with yours. When you feel that the spirit is "on" you, as far as it will go, then you will be at a critical threshold.

If you are new to this, you may feel the impulse to say or do something, and at the same time not know what it is the spirit wants or needs. It is at this point that you, the medium, must give voice to the spirit by forcefully saying the accepted greeting of, "May the Lord's peace be here…!" Yes, it is the medium who begins this part of the spirit's training. Your guide must learn to use your voice as his/her mouthpiece, just as you are learning to be inspired and "impulsed" to say the words you are being given in thought by the entity. This is one of the hardest lessons for both medium and spirit alike.

Usually on my one-on=one development sessions I will lay my hands on the shoulders of the medium and bring the communication of the guide to an end after I ask the entity to cleanse their "mount". In the very beginning I feel that these small steps will gradually give both medium and spirit guide more time to feel comfortable and establish stronger affinity with each other. Rather than using names, the recognition should be based on the knowledge of the particular vibration felt and the thoughts within the medium at the time of the guide's proximity.

Now that we've touched that realm of names and identification, let me climb out onto the limb, so to speak. It is quite an area of contention, the providing of names in public or names of responsible parties privy to evil. I have a distinct feeling on this situation. If our calling is to do positive work, development, and heal, then we have no business in fanning the flames of hate and enmity between people. Do we really need to smear the face of the client with details of who is behind whatever attack we're breaking or lifting? This will stir more hatred and keep the "dirty ball" passed from one person to another, continually staining their hands, not to mention loss of strength. If the medium is truly skilled, he/she will mentally force the spirit to collect all of the evil done to the client, empty into the waters, through the vibrations of their hands, and avoid mentioning where or the source of the evil. Why? I could hear the cries now. Well, kind souls, it is more important to help the client and help that errant soul be lifted to higher spirit colleges than to keep them bogged down in a swamp of "tit-for-tat" warfare. This will never help either the medium or the errant spirit to rise, be healed, and continue their development in the Light.

Most importantly, however, is the fact that the sooner this evil is lifted and evaporated into the waters, the sooner justice will be meted out to the offending party. Nothing goes unpaid in the accountability of spiritual behavior. The Akashic Court is merciless when it comes to this. These heavenly juries decide when, how, and where to mete out justice. Many people have difficulty accepting God's clock. The human timepiece rapidly tic-tocs away, while the cosmic grandfather clock barely goes tick.

The vibrational patterns in the heavens, like pieces in a puzzle, must be in place so that at the moment justice is sent, it will be where the offending party will feel the most pain. Often, a person's children, possessions, livelihood, or health, are the instruments of karmic revenge. And, mind you, people always know why their paying the price of their actions. Everyone says, "Woe is me." However, they don't add the why—even though they fully understand the consequences they're living.

For this main reason, I don't like revelation of identities when lifting a dark soul, who could cause more harm by revealing names than thought. We must show faith in the forces that are helping us to break this evil and not badger them for knowledge that may cause a block to progress.

Now for the guides in your Spirit Quadrant. All of our entities have reincarnated from other lives. Our Quadrant brings souls who still identify with their last incarnation. Whether they were male or female will color their outlook on issues. Since all of us will incarnate in both male and female lives, this aspect of your guides must be respected.

Cultural bias is another quirk your spirits will show time and again. Remember, they're coming off a life that probably has nothing in common with you. Other religions, traditions, foods, dress, and the like will round out how each entity comes through. The medium should teach the Quadrant's souls to have two names—the one for the public, and the real one between the medium and the spirit. This is for security. There are individuals quite adept at causing havoc in another medium's quadrant, to the point of inertia!

There are various ways the spirit could greet a congregation in a misa. They could say, "la Negra", "el Indio"", etc. The vibrations are what should be recognizable to the medium, along with the thought patterns associated with each particular spirit.

How to diplomatically handle this depends on those officiating the misa. One must remember that there are people out there who cannot be given certain information because they will take matters into their own hands and do bodily harm, or worse, to others, once they leave the misa. We must be sure to see to it that the results of a misa reflect positive, profound learning, and a love for peace and unity. Having been in misas that have degenerated into shouting matches, and a few into boxing bouts, I don't relish the idea of giving the client exact information that can be traced and acted upon. Trust the spirits to clean, and take your "case" before the Akashic Court. Trust me, no one dishes out justice as mercilessly as Our Maker!!!

AFRICAN MADAMAS: SALT OF THE MIDDLE PASSAGE

Here we arrive at one of the topics dearest to my heart. These ladies represent the backbone of the mediumnistic world, particularly in Hispanic society. Just listening to the words, "La Madama", brings a myriad of emotions ranging from love, hate, laughter, and respect. These are spirits that descended from female slaves brought to the Americas sailing through the Middle Passage. This route was the shipping lane from tropical western Africa to the West Indies and North America. There were other major routes from Africa's western coast to South America, as well. I will concentrate on the Middle Passage because of the sheer number of slaves that were carried on these ships, as well as the much harsher treatment by owners of slaves, particularly in the United States. The absolute separation and torture in North America far exceeded the rest of the Americas.

It is said that were you to sail the west-bound Middle Passage, you might think your mind was playing tricks on you, much like a mirage in a desert. Faint sounds of singing would tease your ears. This song is the lament of the thousands of slaves who jumped into the Atlantic Ocean to drown rather than submit to enslavement. Of these, the vast majority were women with their children. Rather than go through the pain of seeing their children separated from them forever to exist in chains, they preferred to return to the Mother of the World: Yemaya... Goddess of the Sea, patroness of motherhood, children, families, and stability.

Many names were attributed to Yemaya in the Western Hemisphere. Lemanja, Yemonja, Mamajoe, Mamayeya, to name a few. Each country or region had its own distinct culture and dialect. Illiteracy, isolation, and abject poverty contributed to the birth of these names. I will use primarily Yemaya for the sake of unanimity.

The Madamas. Boy, does this subject sometimes turn people to argue in the United States! The American black was, for the most part, brought up to view the elder women in the family as "Mammie", "Nanna", or "Girl".... These names were always meant to denigrate the black women. As a result, American blacks came to view these titles as offensive and demeaning. Indeed, God forbid you used the brand name of pancakes best known in this country—Aunt Jemima!!!

However, in Latin America this did not evolve that way. Quite the contrary. Madamas were well known for their knowledge of healing, prediction, and removing of evil. However, there is also the fact that they were quite adept, those that had Spirit Quadrants, at causing harm to their enslavers through illness or death! They were, and still are, viewed as symbols of luck, health, money, and spiritual power. Madamas are revered as the salt of the earth. Thus, their souls rise from the briny deep of the Middle Passage to bring comfort to those in need. On the other side of this coin, so to speak, is their clamor for justice against evil! During misas, it is quite rare, indeed, to have a

Madama lifted for being in the Darkness. Ninety-nine percent of the time, Madamas will be there in Light and Justice, true warriors and healers...

The reader might be asking, "What about the Madamas that never left Africa?"

There is barely any difference in the way they intervene on behalf of the living. Black women everywhere exude pride in themselves as women, and as matriarchs. History has shown us the existence of all-female armies in past kingdoms on the African continent! Farming, the source of nourishment from the soil is a woman's domain in the majority of black Africa. Some areas will not touch any land that was worked on by any male, believing it to be cursed. We can loosely connect this to the ancient European practice of blessing a piece of land for fertility. A circle of elders would gather around the couple that were to copulate on the ground. As soon as ejaculation and orgasm occurred, they were to deposit these reproductive fluids on the earth itself. Not too different, after all, except in cultural outlook.

Madamas have a knack for breaking monotony at any misa. Their hard-core humor, often sarcastic and bittersweet, comes in comments once they have mounted their mediums. They usually use this to break up any super sad moments that have occurred during the misa. These comments should be kept short by the mediums. While the Madamas are allowed to get away with this in a misa, mediums should educate their Madamas to keep it to a minimum. Many a misa has been brought to howls of laughter resulting from jokes that sometimes come at the expense of a person, or the very medium of the spirit!

Madamas are so beloved and respected that they are the few souls that can get away with this in any misa. After all, humor is food for the soul, and in this life of injustice and pain, no one knows this better than the ladies who are the salt of the waters of life: the Madamas.......

LIFTING DARKNESS AND SPIRITUAL CLASSROOMS

This, my sibling mediums, is one of the most dangerous and sometimes controversial of all the spiritual skills anyone can possess. Picking up a dark entity, forcing it to lift its negativity, and having your guardian spirits escort it to the "spiritual college in the heavens" is no easy feat… You are given this feared responsibility at birth. You have it or you don't!

Feared? You do well to understand that any time a medium is lifting an evil or negative spirit from a client he/she will always feel afraid. In your gut, you know that this is dangerous stuff. If not ready, the medium might not be able to return from the trance. There are many of these that have joined other mediums in the psychiatric wards being treated, unsuccessfully, for schizophrenia!

Never, ever should a medium attempt this accompanied by only the client. This is always done within the protective circle of the mesa blanca—the misa. Being surrounded by a chain of protective spirits from the other Spirit Quadrants, the medium's own Quadrant will be strengthened to complete the task of cleansing the offending spirit plus the client, and assuring that the medium's guardian spirits do likewise.

Since there is no trial period to master this event, no new medium should attempt this, whether they wish to impress others and satisfy their ego. Huge act of stupidity! Unfortunately, when developing flowering spiritists, I have run into too many that want to fly, rather than walk. Channeling spirits should never be seen as something romantic, entertaining, or to impress.

The client's life is being directly affected by this negative spirit's actions. Their daily existence could be impacted in areas of health, familial relationships, love, and obstruction to their spiritual development. That is why, when a medium is lifting a dark entity off a person in the misa, I demand that everyone pay strict attention, direct their silent prayer for both the client and the medium, and not speak to others during this act.

During the lifting of the negative spirit, the medium will start passing hands over his/her head, reeling in the energy of things that were done against the client. The spirit will speak as the medium keeps cleansing and palming the lip of the water receptacle. This is done as many times as possible until the spirit leaves all of the crippling energy in the waters. Then the medium will help the spirit say, "May the peace of the Lord be here." At this the people mutter, "And with your spirit."

Then the spirit is lifted off of the medium as it fans the aura behind their neck. Immediately the attending medium will call on the working medium's guardian angels. One of them must come. When they arrive and give their greeting, they will then give their medium the passes and clean them in the waters, too. Once done, then all the parties can sit. Usually there will be a call for the Our Father, Hail Mary, and Glory be to God prayed in loud voices. On to the next case...

Misas usually last around three hours. They can be a bit less or a lot more in time, depending on the type of cases that are present. If you begin a 7 p.m., you should be done by midnight. Try not to go beyond midnight, if possible. The energy is not quite the same, especially when you have tired, hungry, and thirsty people present.

This is why at all misas there should be soft drinks and snacks. The energy levels are depleted after a misa, and nourishment is necessary before anyone undertakes their drive home safely. Never have alcoholic drinks on hand to serve. Not even beer. Soft drinks or juice are perfect. Remember that your guests are driving home and shouldn't be put at risk for legal problems—at least not by you. When it comes to food, snacks such as sandwiches, freshly cut fruit, or any pasta or rice dish will be fine.

At my misas I always send out the invitation or word of mouth for people to bring either the refreshments or the snacks to share after the misa. It's worked out fine for me. Avoid foods that are too heavy, though, as digestion could be affected at this hour of the night.

During the closing of the misa I always announce, in English and Spanish, that no one will discuss anything that went on in the misa. I ask for conversations about every day affairs, friendships, or jokes. Anything but matters of the spirit. This will avoid gossip, misunderstandings, and anxiety.

After all the guests leave, most mediums exercise one of two options. They can begin to replace the waters, clean up and leave everything as if nothing occurred, or, leave everything as is and clean up the next morning.

By the end of a misa, the last thing I want is to continue sweating. Thankfully, my Spirit Quadrant has always asked that, whenever possible, I leave everything as is for the next day. In this manner, they will revisit all of the area of the misa and bless once again the area. They will also clean and remove all previously unseen negativities. Even the leaves or broken plants from the cleansings are left on the floor. The only thing out are the candles of the altar. Those devotional candles are kept on as customary.

The one exception could be the bowl of water on the floor in front of the altar. This is the water where people cleaned and blessed themselves in the beginning of the misa. If there is someone who has Yemaya officially crowned on their head or is a well-known devotee of Yemaya, that person will be entrusted with taking out the blessing water to the front of the house. Onto the driveway, street, or lawn this water will be tossed. The chosen person will then return the empty bowl and put it back in front of the altar—only this time upside-down.

Yemaya is the Goddess of the Sea, and the Mother of the World. Her house, the oceans, encompass four fifths of the world, making hers the largest home of all of the Orishas. Since water is what cleans us, and takes away all evil with the currents, it is to her children and devotees that this task of throwing out the water falls to. In some places I have seen how everyone makes two parallel lines with a space in the middle. Down the middle, with the bowl of water, the person makes their passage, sometimes turning carefully, sometimes to music or the clapping in unison, and out the door. You choose what you are comfortable with.

The used leaves, roots, plants, etc., should be gathered in plastic garbage bags and put into an outdoor garbage bin. You may wish to wash the white altar covering, and refresh the altar with incense or holy water. Do not forget to give thanks to God, the Virgin, and all the Santos, Entities, and Spirits that made your misa effective.

If you are one of those that likes to host misas regularly in their home, because they have room enough, you should space them three to four weeks apart. There are groups that like to meet weekly, or bi-weekly. I am of the thought that there should be time in between for the forces to work, and mediums to replenish their Quadrants with prayer and meditation. Besides, we all have private lives that demand our attention, particularly spouses and offspring!

During these "down" times, the cleansing of the home, spiritually, should be done. It will recharge the positive vibrations of the home and sweep out any lingering shadows of negativity. A candle to St. Michael the Archangel will enhance this cleansing. Red or green will do, as these are his colors. The aftermath of a séance is just as important as the preparedness for one. Never forget it...

COEXISTING WITH THE ENEMY

Tolerance has many definitions in today's society. It means something different for each set of persons that practice any religious faith. Indeed, even the atheists have their own definition of tolerance. More often than not, it is within the family that mediums will meet up with a wall of discrimination. No matter how many TV commercials are aired, what type of lessons are taught in classrooms, tolerance is still pushing uphill towards actual acceptance of its real definition.

As a religious world conflagration continues to engulf major parts of the world, the rise of discrimination and hate dramatically touches our families. It is fueled by the foolish presumption that saddles each religious group: that they have God by the gonads…! Religious fanaticism is every bit as dangerous, if not more, than political extremism. It hits at the very core of the family. No one group is more to blame than others. All religions view mediums with fear—a threat to their control over the population.

Since there is universal knowledge that mediums are born into every society on the planet, the world's organized religions all put up walls of defense and attack those individuals with psychic abilities. They are so misguided….

If all the religions of the Earth accepted mediumship, the opportunity for real peace and understanding would dramatically increase. As mediums pick up positive aspects all people have in common, the different civilizations would have the chance to see each other as they see themselves. All humanity has basically the same needs. We all hurt in the same way for the universal reasons of hunger, thirst, and disease.

Here is the ideal window within which to launch mediums to work together. An increase in coordination would bring all societies much closer to harmony. Every medium would help in the areas they are gifted. Healers would stand alongside doctors. There are areas of the planet that come to mind, such as Brazil, where certain hospitals have both medical and spiritual people examine particularly hard cases. They then trade their findings and mutually agree if this is a true physical situation for the doctors, or if there are definitive signs that it's a task for spirit cleansing. Sometimes there is a combination. The staff work accordingly.

Agriculture is another critical area. Places, like the United Kingdom, are famous for their animal healers. The vibrations of these healers can help keeping animals as well as crops healthy. Prevention through their psychic sight could have mediums detecting any problematic areas or illnesses coming in the future. Science could then have a bit of a head start combating illness or plagues by insects.

But, before I continue with my rosy-hued binoculars, I must wake up to the reality of living within a fanatical world.

Many potentially great mediums have been denied to humanity due to its very real and painful treatment of the unexplainable. Born with this added sixth sense, we are not fully aware of how different we are from others until later in childhood. My travels within the circle of Great Work, La Obra, has me estimating that somewhere between five and ten years of age is the average child's awareness of his/her condition. It is here that we will begin seeing the faces of a variety of reactions.

"Shhh…! Don't you dare say anything like that!"

"You will die and go to hell for this!"

"Stop making up fantasies and lies!"

"You have too much imagination, kid!"

"Don't embarrass me! Just shut up and listen!"

"You need to see the doctor. This isn't normal…"

"We must take them to the church for an exorcism!"

"You're weird…!"

I could go on. Surely you've recognized the essence of these reactions that are flung at a mere child who doesn't quite understand the gift. In rare, happier family circles, there are adult mediums who openly "Work". Upon knowledge, which usually preceded the child's birth, that a new medium was gracing the Earth, all stops are pulled out to hasten the child's development. Their surroundings are love, understanding, and learning, learning, learning…

In today's bookstores and in on-line catalogs many children's literature on psychic matters are displayed for society's kids to enjoy. While they grow up their Spirit Quadrants are enriched and flow ever smoother. The child will benefit from this type of environment in positive development and acceptance of their gift. Also, their uniqueness will be viewed as an asset. A vehicle to help olthers making the long trip on this karmic road called Life.

Approaching adolescence and adulthood the individual will confront much colder and harder walls of irrationality and fear.

Things can turn ugly. A teenager is known to be quite stubborn towards authority figures. They claim that they want things different and they are going to be a better generation than their elders. In reality, however, adolescents are much more prone to follow their peers blindly into a void.

In religious matters, like issues of fashion, habits, and culture, peer pressure squeezes like a vise. Anything that is seen as out of the norm is ostracized and subjected to the worst treatment of discrimination one can imagine. Many young mediums will experience the gamut of put-downs. Ignoring their presence, taunting, and—in some cases—violence are the various vehicles of hate targeting these teenage mediums.

As in the beginning of this chapter, we revisit the magic word: tolerance. In a world of fragility, tolerance is the one trait that can strengthen the very roots of existence. Yet, we listen to event after event that confirms the very lack of tolerant behavior. Indeed, in some areas of the world, fanatical religious sects have actually invaded the homes of mediums and attacked the people living there. Furniture and, of course, the statues and altars have been destroyed!

Sounds too far-fetched? Listen to people in rural South America, Africa, and Asia. Your skin will crawl... Hardly anyone reported at the end of the last century that various Protestant sects in the Pacific islands of Micronesia and the South Pacific were actually at war. Church territories were violently fought over, of course, with the Bible in one hand and a rifle in the other!

Keep wondering if these fanatical sects are bringing us any closer to the "kingdom of heaven"... When it hits you completely, have aspirin ready.

ETIQUETTE IN THE MISAS

Discipline and organization are absolutes in any misa. If these two ingredients are lacking, it will resemble a chicken coop when a lone rooster is set loose inside! The cacophony will be deafening. . .

Seriously, though, there are unwritten rules that apply in any misa. The success of the ceremony depends on the participants adhering to them.

First and foremost, one must know the three basic areas of any typical reunion. The first, and most important step, are the opening prayers. The manner in which these are done set the tone for the ensuing misa. Prior to this opening stage, all the people in the room will be socializing, sharing jokes, and dropping gossip pills onto the conversations. I formally call everyone to take a seat and put on what I call my "warlock face" to set a tone of serious mission. Once everyone is accommodated and hushed, I begin the prayers in a clear voice, and the rest follow my prayers.

There are many ways you can have maximum participation during the prayers. A photocopy of the prayers from the book could be printed up in thin booklets. They are passed out at this time, and collected when prayers are over. Another way

I've seen is for a selected individual with a commanding voice to read aloud as everyone else silently, or in whispers, follows.

There is usually a set order to the prayers. It can vary, depending on the traditions of the person hosting the misa, or the two people working "point" at either side of the altar that faces the group. Here is a suggestion of prayers and their order:

1. Our Father, Hail Mary, Glory be...
2. Prayer at the Beginning of the Misa
3. Prayer for the Mediums
4. Prayer for the Guardian Angels and Protective Spirits
5. Prayer for Peace in the Home
6. Prayer for Those We Have Loved
7. Prayer for Those Who Suffer and Ask for Prayer
8. The "Plegaria del Naufrago" (Prayer for a Lost Soul in the Sea of Life)
9. Act of Loving God (Acto de Amor a Dios)
10. Contemplacion (Contemplation)

Again, this is a suggested list. You may add others that provide a positive vibration to the gathering. Prayers that bring out the best in us. But, know this. These ten are staples of the prayers and must be used. The order could change, but these implorations must be prayed.

Once the prayers are done and the booklets are passed down or collected by selected individuals, the person closest to the light switch will turn the lights off. There will not, repeat, not be total darkness in a misa. Prior to the misa there should have been one or two very soft lights placed strategically that people may see, but no glaring overhead lights. Just enough soft light—like a night lamp—that will provide privacy and still let all know and see what is happening.

At this point, the singing begins. A designated person, with a good singing voice, is usually leading the songs, and the rest follow. While the songs are being sung, in a clockwise direction, every person will go up in front of the altar and bend down to clean their auras with the prepared waters. They give themselves the passes with some of the water that they will sprinkle as they clean themselves. Each person should take no more than a minute. Most people will do this rather quickly. Mediums, however, might take a few extra minutes because their spirit quadrants will come very close and they will get the chills, jolts, and may shake and rattle a bit, too. There should always be attention that no one falls.. The floor or mat could get wet, so have a mop nearby.

The songs are usually the ones handed down over the ages by other mediums. You can also have song books. Hymns. Poetic singing. It is up to your tradition.

When the people are going up to clean their auras, there is a pecking order, so to speak. If children are either at the misa, or playing and being watched in another part of the house, the children go first, from the youngest and finishing with the oldest. Any pregnant women will follow, and then the clockwise order will kick in. Looking toward the altar, the table is the 12 on any clock.

Once finished, this first part melts into a second, rather short, second plateau. All those that have received visions during the prayers will say the words, "With the table's permission." Table meaning the one or two people on point that are charing the misa. They will say what they saw briefly, and if they wish, can tell who is the person for whom that vision applies. It will go on like this for roughly five minutes. The chairperson will then indicate the member of the gathering that should come up to the altar and step three has begun in earnest!

Within this process, the chair or point persons will call up to the altar the person whose vibrations hit first onto the table, meaning the mediums. The person will be asked to clean themselves briefly in the prepared water again, and turn around to face the crowd or remain facing the altar. This depends on how the chair wants to work it.

People will then be asked that all those that "see" what's on them speak out. As the mediums, and even some who are not mediums, take turns in saying what they pick up on this, the first patient, the Work starts forming. Once there is an agreement, more or less, on the problem, the medium who can lift evil off will begin. This could be any medium with this capability. There is always one particular one who begins to react with jolts and crawling skin that is obviously being called for this.

Calling on their Quadrant to have a guardian spirit enter, salute, and prepare the aura of the medium is the safest way to achieve the lifting of the entity. Then, as the guardian retreats, the rest of the Quadrant brings through the negative spirit. Concentrated, silent prayer is essential for the protection of the medium. Only one of the mediums conducting the misa should interrogate the spirit. All others should direct any questions that might come up through the filter of this one interrogator. Every orderly step should be taken so as to stop the dark spirit from slipping through or lying.

Here is an extremely simplified example of what could occur:

Interrogator: Give the proper greeting, dear spirit, and remember not to mistreat the body of the medium that has been lent to you. Listen to those good spirits of light that are holding you here.

Spirit: They say I have to say may the peace of the Lord be with you.

Interrogator: And with your spirit. Clean and pick up all of the negatives you are putting on this person. (The spirit will begin cleaning the aura of the medium and 'depositing' into the special receptacle of water for this purpose.)

Spirit: Here is the pain I've inflicted on her. Here is the articles used to send the discomfort. (The spirit is picking up the vibrational life of the objects and neutralizing them by depositing into the waters. The hands of the medium don't actually touch the water ever. The vibration released through the palms of the hands onto the top lip portion of the glass bowl are how the waters pick up the magnetic evil.)

Interrogator: Make sure there is nothing left. I see a red ribbon in knots, twisting their nerves to no end.

Spirit: Yes, here is the ribbon. There is no more. These other souls tell me I must say may the peace of the Lord be with you.

Interrogator (and others): And with your spirit.

Spirit: They are taking me to the spiritual schools. They say I will be helped. Please give me bread.

Interrorgator will then recite the Our Father, Hail Mary, and Glory be—usually accompanied by all in attendance. The medium will then use the palmns of their hands to clean themselves into the waters of any impurities that could have been left behind. Then their guardian spirit must come through, greet, and retreat, as they say, three steps back and say at the service of the medium.

That, in very simplistic terms, is the basic course of action of collecting a "causa", or negative. The medium could be left rather drawn out of energy for a while. This is the reason that, for reasons of health, no more than three "causas" in any given misa should a medium work. At the end of the misa, or upon reaching home, the medium should spiritually clean themselves very well, and shower well, regardless of the time of night or day.

This is no piece of cake, people. It drains your energy. It's also the main reason that food, either snacks or a hot dish, is served afterwards. This gives everyone a chance to replenish their strength before the drive home.

All who come to the misa should contribute with soft drinks or snacks. In most cases the host or hostess might provide a strong main plate.

Since we're discussing etiquette, there are glaring things one shouldn't do. In my lifetime I have been witness or participant of rather horrendous incidents in misas. Some have actually shut the work down and everyone has been sent on their way! These are the misas you need to really clean yourselves from upon arriving home.

Cell phones!!! Oh my God, if I could count the number of times this offensive object interrupted a reunion, I'd go into the "gazillions"…! Rule of thumb dictates you, at least, put it on vibrate. In reality, turn it off! If you have children at home, then leave it on vibrate. However, if the cell phone vibrates, excuse yourself and go outside if you absolutely have to answer it.

When leaving your chair for any reason, something should occupy the chair. This could be a purse, a flower, a cigar, a book, etc. All chairs should be occupied by a person or object. Empty chairs should be folded and put away.

Who told anyone that a misa is a boxing ring?

I have seen and experienced many a confrontation during a misa. It is always a sad sight, generating enemies, gossip, and spirit warfare down the line. Divergent forms of spirit vision will often put mediums at odds with each other or a person from the "audience" could oppose what they have been told.

Keep in mind that not everyone appreciates hearing the truth. If you're the type of person that dislikes being worked on in public by mediums, do not attend a misa. Inclusive, there are individuals out there who will outright deny any true vision you see for them because it isn't in their selfish interest to admit to it. Advice to all mediums, especially those in the beginning stage of development: a person will often give you their side of the story, conveniently omitting parts that do not play out on what they want from the spirits.

Go with your gut instinct, and trust your spirits. The first impression is usually the correct one. When I've confronted a client with the truth of a situation, whether in their favor or not, most people will then admit to what the truth is. Everything is in your delivery. A positive slant on your words is important.

Tact and diplomacy will pay off. Then the client will be more than cooperative in wanting to settle things the right way.

On the other hand, there are obnoxious people out there who will argue and sarcastically or loudly deny what you vision says. These are folks that, if it doesn't fit their pre-conceived notions of what the truth is, they don't want to hear it. Whenever I come across of them, I now either run the other way or ignore their presence completely! That type of human has no place in a misa or a reading.

The worst of the situations usually comes when polarizing views occur between mediums. Oh boy, these are real clashes of egos!

Medium A might see a situation that couild be solved in a particular way. This, mind you, is an "evidencia", vision, given by their spirit guides. Medium B, though, says that the real root of the problem lies elsewhere and proceeds to give a totally different vision of the solution. If not checked diplomatically and forcefully by the chairing medium, A and B could fall into an actual shouting match. I have seen two people disagree and compete to an extreme that they have actually had a fist-fight!!! Trust me, an incident like this calls for the immediate suspension of the misa. The chair should demand the two offending mediums, regardless of who's right, leave immediately.

Then there should be a voiced apology by the hosting medium and all mediums should take turns cleaning themselves and all present to remove any of the negative sparks that flew onto anyone. The presiding medium may ask if the attendees with to carry on the misa or close out. Depending on the hour and severity of the confrontation, most will opt to continue. If so, the misa will restart with a few prayers so that the Quadrants can link up again peacefully and the Great Work continue, uninterrupted by out of control messiah complexes.

There is no doubt that incidents such as these account for many leaving the spirit scene. The vibrations left in their wake darken the atmosphere of the home in which it occurred, forcing the home owners to spiritually clean the home quite heavily. This way, the air will be cleared once again.

As a medium one has to be quite diplomatic and sensitive when informing an individual that there are problems in their life that are caused by either themselves or those dear to them. Measure your words and don't take your eyes off the person. Observe every reaction and body language that will inform you if this person is ready for deeper revelations or if you need to polish the information over to a palatable shine that they can swallow.

Yes, there can be more than one solution to any problem. Often the reality is that there is more than one source of friction in a person's life. Mediums need to look deeply when there are different stories popping up.

Cooperation is the name of the game. Forget not that in a misa, as well as life, everybody knows something and nobody knows anything...

FOOL'S GOLD

We've all heard "all that glitters isn't gold". One only has to look at the pages of local newspapers, magazines, and supermarket gossip rags to appreciate the huge number of psychic advertising. I will tell you right now—over ninety-eight percent of these advertisements are from charlatans!

The world at large is in such a frustrated state that people will go any lengths to get their way. Humanity today is overflowing with selfish, spoiled "children" in adult clothing. Precisely this character flaw is what's driving this flock of lemmings over the edge into an abyss of fraud, lies, theft, and, sometimes, violence. These junkies of the spiritual world are hooked on being told that what they wish for is coming. When they see it doesn't quite pan out, they run to the churches, where they're told salvation will come. When that doesn't occur, they go and try the so-called metaphysical professors—a heady name for witch doctors. Then there are the alternative medicine circles, made up largely of people who wouldn't dare admit they love the spirits. God forbid their friends and family should know!

Within our mediumnistic circles we also have experienced the presence of the anointed ones, flaunting their messiah complex in misas. We even have our share of "Flash Gordons", male and female, who will pass spirits and lift evil at the speed of machine guns, thereby not allowing anyone else to work and deny their credit as saviors.

Once again, I refer the reader back to the phrase used daily in spiritist circles, "Everyone knows something, and no one knows anything…!" This is a folksy way of advising everyone to be humble. In a misa God and the powers that be can choose to use anyone. Veteran mediums, children, and people who have never even felt a vibration can be used to see or to work. The people on point better be prepared for this. Control and discipline in a misa are too critical to tolerate fog.

Another type of charlatan I've had all too many a confrontation with is the one who graciously titles himself as a "botanical worker", dealing out spirit "workings" exclusively through herbs. This individual, who is almost always accompanied by their apprentice, always try to persuade people to buy their "trabajos botanicos".

I know of one who always carried a small, thin wand. He would like to grandstand and use the little wand to tap on the glasses. This was another tactic to keep people mesmerized and attentive as he spoke on about the effectiveness of plants.

Yes, plants all have healing and spiritual qualities. But no one should be expected to shell out money in three or four figures for these "miracle cures"…Honestly, how could anyone be expected not to rebel? The "lambs", that's who! In their quest for instant gratification and cures, humanity will follow any person that projects credibility and salvation.

What many don't realize is the extent to which hypnotic techniques are used. Even Evangelical pastors use these tricks of the trade, so to speak. If you have ever studied Adolf Hitler and Nazi Germany, you observed that the use of hypnotic choreography, speech, and song enabled Hitler to control the otherwise normal families the way he did. Hitler always said that if you repeat a lie enough, it will be eventually believed as truth. He also is quoted as saying, "Humanity is, at best, despicable…"

In the Nuremburg Museum in Germany, one can still see the pronouncement by the Pentacostal church of Germany, declaring Hitler as the Second Coming of Christ…!

All this relates back to the charlatans we have to deal with. Today the global community of mediums is under fire directly from the Evangelical Inquisition, extremist elements of Islam, and Communist regimes. In this environment we can no longer afford to turn the other cheek. We must arm ourselves with factual information to counter the fanatical lies that are flung at us. We must, in addition, lose our good manners, and shout back!

I once had a rather loud, nasty encounter with a fanatical Christian in an all too well known department store. As I was walking from the cashier with my cart, this gentleman sees a particular piece of jewelry associated with spiritism that I've worn over three quarters of my life.

He yells out, "Back, Satan!"

Well…. I lost it. Really lost it.

"Satan lives in your soul, you !@#$$%^&&^*!"

I proceeded to rant on and on into his face. By now we were both beet red and about to come to blows. Security got there quickly and asked us to cool down and exit separate ways. As he murmured under his breath, I answered in my most sarcastic manner. Needless to say, the customers had quite a show that morning!

As time evolves these fanatics are becoming vocal and, sometimes, violent. I would counsel any medium to either take up martial arts seriously, or learn to become a sharpshooter. You may see these viewpoints as extreme and unnecessary. Trust me, no matter how much freedom a person enjoys in any given country, history is full of religious fanatics injecting populations with a fervor of hate and "righteousness"... History has repeated itself all too often. In these times we live in there have been examples of Buddhist attacks on Muslims in Myanmar, physical fistfights among the Pacific Island various Protestant churches, Hindus at war with Muslims, the Communist Chinese attempting to muffle the voice of Tibet's Dalai Lama, and Northern Ireland's strife between Protestants and Catholics. Even worse, Europe's Christian elite has devastated the Gypsy (Roma) population.

The charlatans that the world has to put up with, are contributing to all of this hate and violence. Those of us who labor for true mediumnistic values must be the first line of attack against these charlatans. They have undermined society's trust in us, and tried to have us all labeled as carnival freaks... They are worse than all the rest! Learn to recognize them and work to have them either stop or take up being Protestant ministers, living off tithing... Pastors start poor, but end up quite the opposite.

THE CAVES KEEP WHISPERING

Let us continue with our boveda [BO ve da]. Whether you have a boveda composed of nine glasses or one, your attentive maintenance is important to your growth.

The periodic cleansing of the glass receptacles is a safeguard against psychic attack. These caves of hidden knowledge provide bridges of communication across the aisles of the veil. The water they house should always be clear and magnetic.

First step when cleaning the boveda glasses, once emptied of the old water, is to use salt. Whether it's table salt or sea salt is up to you. Sprinkle heavily the inside of the wet glass, as well as the outside. Secondly, use a very good liquid dish soap. A little bit will do. Finally, use hot water as you scrub and rinse each glass. Put them aside to dry a bit.

Once done, arrange the boveda on the altar the way your spirits indicate while they're still empty. Then use a clean pitcher to pour cold tap water into each one to the top. **Never** use refrigerated or bottled water. The tap water of a house does provide vibrations associated with the home and its occupants. Mediums can often tell all about everyone and the problems in that home from the tap water. It should always be cold tap water.

One issue that always keeps coming up is the location of the caves. Vibration has everything to do with this decision. Trust your instincts as to where your spirit guides want the boveda [BO vay dah]. Usually they will steer you towards a corner from which they can oversee the room. Your spiritual quadrant will use the boveda to pick up unwanted energies, to contain info to be used by you at a later time of prayer and meditation. In fact, there are resident entities whose task it is to keep the caves drawing in energy from all who visit or live in your home. Hence, the waters that often cloud up or fill with bubbles of negative energy. When the top of the water receptacles has a ring of bubbles around the top, like a crown, that is a sign that all is positive in the area.

We now come to the glass caves outdoors. A boveda that is put outside in the back yard of a home is always prescribed by the quadrant. Due to the presence of specific entities, you will be directed to put up this second boveda outdoors. Spirits that deal with the astral plane, those that come through the Palo Mayombe religion, and Indigenous Indians are entities that will probably demand this extra boveda outside of your home. Those mediums that, in addition, are or deal with astrologers will most likely be pressed for this, too.

Choosing the site of this boveda will take deep meditation and prayer to ask for guidance as to where on the property's back yard the spirits wish to center themselves. You may have a small table near a tree or special plant. Since they will be outside, the glasses, or goblets, should not be glass. Here is where there could be controversy with other mediums. Some of you may wish it to be quite folkloric in nature. I know of some outside bovedas consisting of scraped, and shaped coconut half-shells. Many have been clay. Whatever material you choose for the makeup of your boveda is up to your spirits and you. Weather will play a major role in the choice of a material suitable for the climate you live in.

These waters could be changed once a week, depending on the rate of evaporation and what it may have picked up. A daily check of an outdoor boveda is important. Choose a spot where it will be difficult for animals, such as rodents, birds, or reptiles to disrupt it.

Mediums who have astral entities will be quite drawn to this, particularly during the full Moon phases. Likewise, those with entities that work with herbs, roots, and rocks.

Regular periods of five minute meditations will ground your boveda to its surroundings as well as open it to better reception to incoming astral rays from space.

CLOSE ENCOUNTERS

Strong indications of another type of spiritual connection dwell deeply within many mediums. Their calling for a unique form of contact stands out from the rest. I call your attention to all the Indian civilizations of the Americas. Stories of the Star People proliferate through each one. Indigenous people in the Western Hemisphere consider themselves as special guardians of the planet. Hence, their interest in the conservation of Earth's resources.

Many a tribe has pointed to the Pleides star system as their true home. So much archeological studies seem to verify this view. The gigantic carvings on the Pacific coast of South America showing huge spider-like designs that could be landing strips or markers. Different types of pyramids and mounds. The drawings of many Aztec and Maya on temple walls that depict alien space suits or very strange beings.

Expanding further, the so-called "UFO phenomena" is, in reality, a beam of energy forces awakening humanity to something further than our galaxy. There are spiritual and living beings beyond our stars that are doing everything possible to create bridges of communication. They are inspiring our collective consciousness in ways we didn't expect. Literature,

Art, and Cinema have been at the forefront of this push to provide readiness for an eventual public confirmation.

There are several incidents that stand out in my memory of these direct face to face encounters. I will start off with the first of these. All three incidents occurred during the thirteen years I lived in Puerto Rico, a commonwealth of the United States.

My wife and I were driving up a wide highway on a mountainside of Aguadilla, a municipality on the island's northwest corner. To the left of us we could clearly view the ocean hugging the beaches. Having worked in the past for the airline industry before becoming a teacher, I was aware that all aircraft employ outer lights that are green, white, and red. This is universal. As we looked further an object appeared in the night sky. It looked to us like a helicopter of sorts. But then I noticed the lights on it were *blue,* white, and red. As if reading my mind, the object flew straight up into the night sky at breakneck speed!

Struggling not to ride off the mountain highway, my wife and I decided to call the now-defunct Center for UFO Sightings. They came to our home the next day and took down our testimony and essential data. We were told by them what had always been commented about this part of Puerto Rico. It was a location of many reports of UFO contacts, as well as the El Yunque rainforest on the eastern side of the island.

A while later, I was sitting home alone watching TV. I heard our dogs barking at the back door, off the kitchen. I also was starting to receive the chills normally associated with the presence of spirits. However, this felt decidedly strange. I kept feeling a need to walk to the kitchen and open the back door. When I did, I looked at the moonlit sky that only had two small clouds side by side. I thought it was weird that on a perfectly clear night there would be two curiously-shaped clouds. Just then, swoosh! Two dots of light with a trail of white light sped off to the east…! I was stunned… Immediately the chills left my body.

I began analyzing what had just happened and what I'd also experienced in the first incident. Both times I came away with a realization of how advanced their communications are, whoever they are.

The Rosicrucians state that thoughts have wings. This is like a form of radar. It kept recurring that every time I thought concerning sighting the UFOs, they immediately took off. This could only mean that they picked up my thought waves and read their pattern instantly. . . ! It would explain much of what happens when others meet up with these visitors.

My third encounter was very, very different. My madama, had channeled through me and spoken to my wife. She gave the following intriguing directions to her.

"On the evening of—I can't remember the exact date—you will make sure he is home before five in the afternoon. He is going to go into a catalytic state. He will be channeling an entity from far, far away and should be lying down in the temple before then. Have blankets and lots of sweet, black coffee. He will be taken out of the trance every two hours or so. Make sure he wakes up, walks around, and goes to the bathroom before he begins to feel dizzy again. This should be around ten minutes. Make sure he has plenty of coffee, as he'll feel very cold. He will then lie back down on the temple floor, cover him, and he will be returned to the trance. Make sure you have plenty of pencil and paper for the messages and information he will receive…"

Well, you can imagine how *that* was received!

When the date and time finally arrived, I remember feeling oh so dizzy and sleepy. As I lay down on the floor, resting my head on a pillow, I remembered feeling colder and colder. Mind you, Puerto Rico is tropical. It must have been around eighty-five at the time—and muggy. I still shivered with cold. Those who know me well know how I dislike extremes. Neither too hot or too cold. If I have to choose, though, I'll be warm. I do not like cold one bit. When you grow up in the ghetto with very little heat, wet snow curling your toes, and sleeping with coats on, you will understand me.

Suddenly I felt heavy. In my mind I envisioned a beam of green and red light opening and bringing me someone to meet! I didn't quite see this entity, but I could feel his presence. A male figure was clearly present, though not very visible. I found myself being controlled by the thoughts of this being. Every thought he had, I uttered in speech! In English, to boot…! My wife, thank God, is bilingual, a plus on the island.

What follows is a short excerpt of the conversation he had with my wife and a few friends that had been invited as witnesses. I felt like I knew this entity all my life. Comfort filled me and replaced the initial fear I felt at being controlled hypnotically. This is some of Arthur's message:

1. He spoke in English because it was one of the languages that was easier to submit to translation, in addition to Mandarin, Russian, Mayan.

2. His planetary origins were so far beyond our galaxy that the right timing had to be figured so as to be able to relay his vocal vibration. It would take from that

time until about 2021 for alignment to be conducive for another contact.

3. He spoke of coming illnesses for specific friends of ours. These predictions all came to pass.

4. Specific events were forecast, i.e., the beginning of a century of darkness and insecurity, the Great Recession of 2008, and a looming global crisis over water and agriculture. Looking back now, I am stunned.

5. He forecast more UFO contacts, as well as discoveries that extraterrestrials were here long ago. That there are still secret visits occurring.

6. A major point of entry would be discovered at the very depths of our oceans. Ironically, the first public contact would occur beneath the waves!

During all of these messages, I would come out of the catalytic trance with instructions Arthur would give my wife. I had ten or fifteen minutes to have hot, black coffee and visit the bathroom. Shivering with cold—in a hot, tropical climate! I still ponder on the bone-chilling cold I felt. It reminded me of the coldest winter days in New York City, where I grew up. Those tenements back then were ice boxes, especially when the landlords turned off the boilers because they didn't buy enough coal to warm the steam pipes and radiators!

When the allotted time had passed, Arthur announced that the connection was dimming and the session had to end. He gave instructions for my wife to feed me specific vitamins through fruits, vegetables, and fish. I was a bit worn out for a few days after that.

His final statements hinted at a future return, event that hinged on the stability of the Earth today. Further explanation based this event on the approval of the governing council of his planet. His planet's name, like his own, was one we would find almost impossible to pronounce. Should there be excessive war or climatic destruction, the council would put off the contact until the galactic lineup was conducive again. This, if missed around this time, would take it to 2073... Of course, by then Arthur would have to find another contact, as I would be in spirit. Arthur told my wife that I would be in a high plateau in spirit. The possibilities of my reincarnating, he hinted at, would be slim, since I was due to progress towards another level of light.

Whatever thoughts have pierced my mind daily, this incident was one of my most intriguing and troubling occurrences. Troubling in the sense that the knowledge of how small we really are in this universe proves how vulnerable a target we really are. I firmly believe that the world's governments are in league with keeping the global inhabitants in the dark. The very fact that they and the world's main religions could lose control over people is, in itself, scary to both the powers that be as well as to the average individual, whose life will be irrevocably uprooted.

Perhaps my prayers will be answered at some foreseeable moment. There needs to be a determined, but orderly, release of knowledge regarding the visits to Earth by extraterrestrials. There have been too many sightings, videos, and contacts that have slipped through the cracks. It is time to come clean.

DRUMS: HUMAN HEARTBEATS

Stethoscopes mirror the basic instrument of humankind—the drum. As the cardiologist monitors the heartbeats, the drums reflect the throbbing universal heart of Earth. Music has, rightfully so, been labeled as prayer with a tune. If we look at all cultures, we'll find a common denominator. That is the drum, in all of its varieties, shapes, and musical pitch.

At first thought, of course, Africa comes to mind. However, all societies, without exception, possess a representative of this instrument. From the Taiko drums of Japan, to the Celtic hand drums. From the hollowed out tree trunk drums of the Pacific Isles, to the modern Salsa congas of the Caribbean. In fact, everywhere there is life, people's heartbeats are reflected in their music.

My beloved drums. Is there any music without them? None that I know of. The rock band drummer and the tom-tom player have the same common objective: to reflect the human heart, beating alive. Filling the void with the power of the spirit.

Drums very often have a sacred place within religious rituals. The *Bata* [ba TA] drums are sacred to the Yoruba religion, known also as Santeria. There are three of them. They are always together, each played by a man who is consecrated to the entities that govern these Bata drums. For the layman, their use in any Santeria drumming, *tambor* [tam BOR] in Spanish, is the equivalent of High Mass for Catholics. They are stunning to see and listen to. They literally speak to the participants of any ceremony and are in harmony with the singer who calls the entities in the Yoruba language. To be a part of this men have to go through initiation and study the Yoruba language in detail. Once in a ceremony, there is no paper to read from! Anything less than pure memory and inspiration will not be tolerated at any drumming...

I have used the Bata drums as a brief glimpse into the divinity of their presence. Music without drums, in whatever form or volume, is like a microphone that's turned off.

You can also provide drums, actual or model size, to your worship area. I have an African drum that was given to me by my late mother and father, be in Light, as a Christmas gift! Boy, did I ever get surprised on that Christmas!

MY VEHICLE, MY BLANKET

One would think this would be the last thing in a spiritual book, but no. When behind the wheel, your spiritual radar is at its sharpest. The world is full of real life testimonies of spiritual events while driving. With the incidents I have experienced, and those of so many others I know, there is no doubt in my mind that our guardian angels also possess a driver's license!

"Wearing" your vehicle occurs the second you start it up. While driving our senses are on high alert. You are always conscious of safety. The traffic lights. Stop signs. Yield. Pedestrian crossings. Railroad tracks. School zones. And the list can be elongated endlessly. As a result of this physical state, your spiritual quadrant is alert to any problem that could interfere with destiny. In other words, any action by you or the other drivers that would cause, for instance, your life to be cut shorter than designed. The spirits' intervention takes many forms. Here are just a few, beginning with what I know best......my own.

During the 1970s I was dating my fiancée, who is my wife of over 40 years as of this writing. Back then we lived on the northwestern coast of Puerto Rico. She lived in Aguadilla, and I lived in another town, Isabela. It was between a thirty and forty minute drive. The route went through winding small roads that snaked through small mountains. That area of the island is on a plateau almost as high as the central mountains.

We were having a rather fun conversation with her parents which made everyone forget the clock. It was a weekday and I should have been leaving at around ten. When we finally glanced at the time, it was around 11:30 or so. We all said our good nights, her parents went off to their room, while my wife and I said our good nights—and the rest of it—and I left around midnight.

I remember how tired and sleepy I was. Elvia and I studied at night and it sapped a lot of energy from us. All I remember was turning onto the main road to go home...*My snoring* woke me up in front of my house in Isabela! My foot was on the brake and the transmission was in neutral!

Still in a bit of a stupor, I put the car into "drive", and parked in the driveway. When I entered the house it hit me... **Who drove my car?** I racked my memory and came up blank. Nothing arose in my thoughts of how I drove through those hills with traffic lights and stop signs. I was resting in bed thinking. I couldn't regain my sleep. Finally, I began to receive vibrational thoughts as to what happened.

I was shown a darker pair of hands on the steering wheel. They covered mine with a transparency that allowed me to see both holding the wheel in the exact same place and position. I was being shown flashes of the drive. I knew then that a spirit guide had "driven" me home safely. I immediately swung out of bed and approached by altar, giving prayers of thanks and blessings.

On another occasion, during an evening class, I started getting so sleepy my head was bobbing. I dreaded having to drive late back home, so I excused myself with the professor and left. I drove straight home and went to bed soon after. The time was 9:30 p.m.

Classes ended at ten that night. Meanwhile, I was dreaming of a particular friend, whom I'll call Oscar. In this short dream, I was in the back seat of his car and all I could see was that I was talking to him, as he looked at me through the rearview mirror. It was a short dream and I just kept sleeping.

The next night when I went to class, Oscar waves and calls out he needs to see me right away. It sounded like a problem.

"Freddie, you won't believe how you saved my life last night!'

"What do mean? I was out like a light at home by 9:30."

"I was driving home around 10:30. I got all kinds of chills and when I looked in the mirror—there you were in the back seat of my car!" Oscar then proceeded to really cause my hairs to stand on edge. "You told me, as clear as day, to get out of the road and turn off the car because another car without lights was speeding behind me and would hit me and cause my car to go off the road into a tree."

"What happened?"

"I did just as you said. A few seconds later, swoosh!!!, a car with no lights sped down the road like a bat outta hell…! Those were your spirits, bro…"

We then sat down and studied this event in detail. The only thing that could have occurred is that during my sleep, I had traveled to him and spared him from a horrid accident. Astral projection.

Cars. If they could talk, my, my, my, the world would really blow up!

Over the years I've heard and witnessed so many odd happenings on the road, that I'm over the shock value.

I remember reading about a terrible crash that resulted in both cars twisted like pretzels and everyone perished, except the baby that was in his mother's arms. What was truly the headline of this story was the fact that the infant flew out of the window!!! The child landed on bushes, still wrapped in blankets, and his cries were what alerted bystanders to his location. It was hard to grasp in their minds, how this baby was unscratched in an accident where all died and the cars looked like the aftermath of a bomb blast. And to have seen that baby literally thrown out of the window of the moving vehicle was just too much for many there.

Of course, what happened was simple to the mediumnistic eye. The baby's guardian angel literally catapulted him out. His destiny was not to die so young. This young soul must now be an estimated 30-year-old man. Bless him wherever he is today.

There are blessings that are performed on our vehicles. These rituals are simple and require only one essential: *faith...!* To those who might be snickering I refer you to the masters of spirituality, Asians. All too often I have come across newspaper and magazine photos depicting the blessings of cars, machinery, appliances, computers, as well as most manufactured equipment and goods. These photos may include a Shinto, Taoist, Hindu, or Animist elder in the process of bestowing a blessing to the finished products so that they will sell and bring prosperity. When we all realize how successful this area of the world is, the snickers are silenced by cold reality.

Here are some examples of vehicular blessings:

1. Lighting a cigar, which you will blow its smoke onto the outside of the car, particularly the area of motor and tires. Using a red or red and black kerchief that has been soaked in prepared potion that is made up of herbs, alcohol, and Florida Water, you will "fan" the outer body of the car without touching it. On the inside, the smoke is blown onto the steering wheel and in every seat in the car. This includes the motor itself and the trunk. Make sure the motor is turned off. With the Kerchief, fan the inside, also. During this entire cleansing of the car's aura, the Lord's Prayer as well as a prayer to Eleggua should be recited repeatedly until finished.

2. Catholic rosaries are used extensively by spiritists. They are hung on the rearview mirror. Even mediums that are Protestant use them. I have seen car blessings hanging from rearview mirrors that reflect Judaism, Hinduism, Islam, Buddhism, and any and all religions. These objects are cleansed in holy water and used once being consecrated through prayer.

3. Statuettes of various religious representations are another form of blessing a car that has always enjoyed popularity. A Crucifix, or St. Christopher are mainstays in this. Other saints can be used, depending on the owner's devotion. A note here about St. Christopher. He is not just the patron of travel, but is also a saint that carries us over the waters of pestilence as he did the Christchild. Another big patron of health.

4. Still another form of spiritual blessing for vehicles are kerchiefs that are tied in a knot over the rearview mirror. These are blessed at home first. Make sure that the actual kerchief does not ever obstruct the view. It will prevent a ticket.

Many times other people's negative vibrations or curses can lock onto our cars like an unwanted GPS beam. Culprit par excellence of this? Lending one's vehicle. Boy, oh boy! This can open up a nasty can of worms that will haunt the owner long after the borrower returns your wheels. My set policy on this comes down to educating myself about who I am lending my car to.

First and foremost, however, do I really need to do this? Is the reason for lending my car to another driver a matter of emergency? Does this situation have an alternate solution that doesn't involve my wheels?

Once that's been decided and in favor of lending, my next step is to make sure I know as much as possible about the driver. If they're a family member or very close friend, of course, immediately I'll know if this request is legit and not an excuse to see "third party" on the sly! Try to find out as much as possible about events leading up to their situation.

I will then bless the car with a prayer, discreetly out of the person's sight. Once the car is returned, I will then spiritually clean the car and bless it. If there were any type of legal, health, economic, or romantic issues, let these leave with the person in question and not vibrationally infect the car's aura.

Paranoia? *NOT...* After all I've experienced and seen involving cars, curses, and cures? No chances of skipping this step.

It is always good to pray at least the Lord's Prayer as soon as you start the car for the first time in the day. It will set a protective shield around you and the vehicle that you're wearing. Enjoy the drive....

REVISITING ETIQUETTE

In my first book I dealt with the phenomenon of spiritual etiquette during rituals, readings, and misas. I feel it quite necessary, given the social laxity of today, to touch on this in detail once more.

The misa is one of the most important events to observe etiquette in the spiritist world. Most people will dress in white, but light pastel colors are fine. As for the ladies, it is understood they can wear dark or black skirts during particular times, given their menstrual cycles. There are spirit houses where it is not permitted or women to attend who are menstruating. I don't hold to that. As long as she brings materials for her comfort, she is more than welcome in my misas. However, always check with the host, rather than go through an awkward moment publicly.

While we're on attire, I would like to address the gentlemen in the audience. Guys, if there's any place **not** to wear sagging pants, it's in a misa. When people go up to the altar to clean themselves, they must bend down to do it. We don't need mooning at this moment. Once, I hate to even remember, there was a man who we all saw the stain on his underwear!!! Don't ask…

Both genders should wear blouses and shirts that have sleeves, don't show cleavage or too much chest, and no printed slogans that require a rating of Mature Audiences only. No low backs, tank tops or shorts. Definitely no miniskirts.

As for skirts versus pants, women need to check with the host on the house rules. Me, I have no requirement for skirts. However, skirts are a must for any woman who is in the Santeria or other African-based religions. Simple rule of thumb: when in doubt, a knee-length or long skirt.

One must always keep at the forefront of our thoughts that the objective is to work with the spiritualistic body, not the physical. So, ladies, don't wear clothing that outlines your figure. This is why most places demand knee-length or long skirts.

During the prayers it is most appreciated when all pray in a regular tone of voice. In some places, though, they will assign someone to read the prayers aloud. Those that know the prayers well, can recite them with the reader or silently listen and concentrate on the message they convey.

Once the prayers are over, most places will sing established spiritual songs. While this is occurring, one by one, all will go up to the altar and stoop to put their hands on the water, give themselves passes, then sit again. There is a strict order to be followed here. Children, youngest to oldest, go first. Pregnant women next. Then the adults.

Once everyone has cleansed themselves, it's the cue to sing the last song. Now we enter that small second step of the misa. Here the mediums will briefly state whatever visions they received during the prayers. Remember, even those who are not full-fledged mediums are attending because they were called there. If they see something they should say it. Proper manners are observed by the individual medium saying, "With the permission of the table (meaning the two people on point) I wish to say ….." Then they would proceed to briefly state their vision to the point.

At this moment, when those mediums that saw have spoken, a small silence ensues and then the president of the table or the persons on point begin by calling for the Lord's Prayer out loud. The third and final portion of the misa has begun.

This is where, as I detailed in <u>Mesa Blanca</u>, hard work takes place. The mediums on point, although it could be any medium in the group, will ask someone to stand up, approach the altar, quickly clean themselves and face the group. The medium will begin to identify what they see, hear, or feel toward him or her. We shall call this person "A" to avoid redundancy. As the medium continues to tell "A" the things that were seen, "A" should answer "Luz", if in Spanish, or "Light", if in English. This is a way of ascertaining the medium's accuracy as to what they picked up. It also bestows an abbreviated blessing of thanks towards the medium's Spirit Quadrant. This inspires the medium and the Quadrant to move forward.

Others may have additional visions to say, and they should ask permission to speak and then let the originating medium continue. Here the medium might be getting up and passing their hands along the aura, cleaning it by "dumping" negative vibes into a water receptacle that is specifically on the table for this purpose. It could be a wide bowl, or, preferably, a low, round goldfish bowl. This is always in addition to the water used to divine on the altar.

After the cleansing is done, or any dark entity has been lifted, the person will be asked to sit and the misa moves on to the next case.

Now comes my **absolute** pet peeve during any misa. While one person is being worked on, the rest need to concentrate their vision as well as their prayers on the person being worked on. This is not the time to chit chat or comment on someone's fashion statement. All cell phones should have been turned to vibrate or off. Unless you know it's your children's babysitter, you can leave it be. If you are the type who must answer, then excuse yourself, leave an object of any type on your seat, and take the call outside.

Why the object in your absence? Keeping the seat occupied with yourself or with an object of yours, i.e., keys, purse, book, is a sign to the spirits of who is there. During a misa one should never change one's seat unless absolutely necessary.

Please don't chitchat with one another. If you see something for another person, have the patience to wait until they are finished with the person in front of the altar. When there are two or more mediums doing their thing on their own, it cuts into the vibrations of the others. This can create confusion and allow truly evil entities to influence the misa.

The word in a misa is: control.

During readings, it is polite to await the medium's instructions as to how they do their readings, and you follow accordingly. It is best for the client to leave questions for last so loose ends can be tied. Mediums have their own particular way of structuring their readings. I have the person place their left hand over the water of a small goblet I have on the table. The hand will sent vibrations into the water, enabling me to see in the water, as well as the aura. Left hand is my Spirit Quadrant's choice.

Next, I'll have the client hold the book of prayers by Allan Kardec in their hands and open it wherever they wish. I immediately insert my hand on the page to prevent it from closing, and read the title of the prayer they opened up to. I may have to go back a few pages if they opened in the middle of a prayer. The title of the prayer will set a tone for the reading.

Afterwards, I use my Tarot cards in a 12-card horoscope spread. This allows me to address every area of the client's life. As a reinforcement, I throw the Runes, to underscore what came out in the reading.

If a spirit chose to come through this might be the best time. If the person is a regular in spiritual circles, they will understand how to speak with a spirit that has possessed me. If I am told they have never experienced this, I call in my wife so she could monitor, translate, and deliver the message properly.

Regardless of the structure, the tools used, or the setting, every medium has their own set style of reading the public. All of these differing forms are legitimate, as long as you are in the company of a truthful psychic. It pays to ask beforehand about paper, recordings, etc.

May your Light guide you to readers that will truly and honestly illuminate you and help you in your endeavors.

May the peace of the Lord be with you.....

DISASTERS ARE THE RESULT OF STUPIDITY!

More often than I care to recall, I'll either pick up a newspaper or turn on the TV news channel to a horror story concerning some charlatan causing a tragedy. Using your God-given brain and common sense is, unfortunately, a commodity in today's day and age. One thing we all must have clarity on, is the relationship between science, spirit, and smarts… That third one is particularly lacking, sorry to say.

Most of the potions in the spiritist field contain alcohol. Duh…! Alcohol is highly flammable, right? So why would a charlatan decide she or he is going to cleanse the aura of a baby by wiping the infant down with some Florida water and proceed to pass the child over the flame of a candle? My God!!! The headlines screamed child sacrifice, spooks, witches, cannibalism, orgies—you can just imagine how the tabloids went ape-shit over this…!

Parents were naturally distraught over their baby's terribly burned body. The tragedy took a turn for the worse when, three or four days later, the infant passed away. The spirit world surely was there en masse to receive this soul with open arms and love.

Enraged over this disaster, I tried to keep my composure as I prayed for the child's soul and its parents' suffering. How could the jerk of a charlatan have not known this was going to happen? Everyone with two fingers of a forehead knows what the outcome is of bringing alcohol and fire within close proximity. Bang! Almost like an explosion the bluish flame of Florida water will shoot over any place where it's put. There are rituals that call for Florida water to be burned on the floor and the people carefully jump near it. Of course the floor must be concrete or concrete tile, otherwise—there goes the house…!

Same thing if ladies don't hold their long skirts up, or gentlemen aren't careful with their pants.

These accidents with fire during spirit rituals are not rare at all. Too often there have been small mishaps of little or no consequences. However, many a medium or person attending a ceremony has been severely burned. Please, if you are not sure if something can catch fire, read the label, speak with elders who have worked with fire.

The real problem here is the Messiah Complex. A medium must never delude themselves into thinking that their spirits will make them stronger than the average human. Their power goes to their head, enabling results like the one we are discussing.

Often egos are puffed up beyond logic. The psychic forgets that miracles like walking on water or passing through fire unharmed are reserved for God to hand out. This is a rare occurrence.

Another event, like walking on hot coals, employs scientific methods that amount to self-hypnosis. But the patient can't always do this like a practitioner. Hence, headlines and court cases…

THE SUPERMARKET

Let's go shopping, people! There's only one store that I enjoy shopping in, because I don't walk in alone. My spirits push me through the door… If you remember from my first book, <u>Mesa Blanca: the White Altar</u>, the perfumed aroma emanating from this business establishment is what led me to La Botanica in my early childhood. Those days in the ghetto of the Bronx in New York City seemed filled with wonder and family support. I was too young to realize where I was truly living—yet.

Botanicas represent to the Puerto Rican, Cuban, and Dominican communities that thread of unity that has always united us: the spirit world and its matter-of-fact involvement in daily life. There are other communities who share this, but, at the time of my childhood, these three were the most present communities in my life.

Let's begin a brief tour of this market…

On a typical botanica's wall you will find rows and rows of devotional candles. They are supposed to be seven-day lights. However, there are several reasons that often cause either less or more flame time. When your devotional candle's glass cylinder is turning black and sooty, it's collecting negative energy associated with the purpose that the candle was lit for.

When this occurs, it's best to repeat the ritual. The second time around, the candle should burn clean and relatively clear. Candles should always be lit with a specific goal or petition. Since they can always pick up negative energy they should always be housed in a clear vase, about one third full of water.

I dare anyone to grab one of these candles when their flame is halfway down. You will burn the skin off of your fingers..! I have also had mine blow up or crack. Sometimes this is the way spirits can break a hex that's just too heavy in the environment. This way the candle can be left on, as it is supposed to burn uninterrupted. The burning of candles as little as four or even three days, indicates there is a serious need for your petition to be granted. Here, too, I would suggest a repeating of the dedication of the candle.

What if it takes forever to burn? Great! All is peace and protectiveness for the devotion or petition associated with the candle. I've had them burn as long as ten or twelve days. This speaks of positive energy and blessings.

As we continue walking through the botanica you will run across the area of incense and oils. Owners of botanicas wouldn't be caught dead without a hefty supply of incense and oils. In addition, there are staples such as "cascarilla" [kas ka RI ya]. This is originally made from a mixture of egg shell and chalk. It helps to keep evil entities at bay. Cascarilla is used to draw sigils on floors, as well as markings on skin. It is easily removed with water, which is why it's so popular.

Uses of cascarilla vary. Since it is considered a property of Obatala, owner of all heads, and liberator of chains, seeing it used in court is not rare. When a person needs to come out well or victorious in a court case, they will have had a cleansing ritual done the night before the trial. During that cleansing they will most probably be instructed to scratch the lump of cascarilla with their hands, so that the powder sticks to the underside of the nails. As they enter the courtroom, they will flick their fingers out on the sides so that the powder is let loose, however small the amount. This is to charge the courtroom's aura with vibrations of release.

Word of caution to anyone who fanatically believes that this *has* to produce results. If you are truly guilty, the probability of you going free are small indeed. Though the spiritual forces help us, there are material events, caused exclusively by human behavior, that cannot be interfered with. God's justice will prevail... Sooner or later the gavel will come down. Word to the wise. Don't push the hand of God if you know you're guilty. Better yet, ask for mercy and a lightening of the sentence or probation.

Next in the botanica is the area of jewelry, beads, chains, and various other tools of the spiritual path. All of the items here are, as a rule, unblessed so that they are adapted to the needs of the practitioner. In some botanicas that cater to santeros you will find necklaces of the saints that have been fed. By fed I mean there has been blood sacrifice on them so the "collares" [ko YA res] are not in need of any further blessing, thus they are ready to be used in the ritual. The necklaces are never to be bought by an uninitiated person. You invite disaster. The person who should purchase them is the santero who is going to initiate you in the ritual that can span all day or three days of preparation. You may give the money to the santero to buy them, or you can accompany the santero to the botanica.

There is a sizable bloc of santeros who make their own necklaces. Just remember one thing: the string MUST be #10 COTTON... Every time I see necklaces threaded with plastic I want to choke whoever did them and worse to those that dare sell these to the public as real. Legitimacy is a commodity that must be preserved!

One more spot at most botanicas is the consultation room. Many botanicas do readings for the public. Some people prefer going far, where they aren't seen entering a botanica for a reading. It has its good side, as well as its negative element.

I tried my hand at reading in a botanica twice. I never lasted more than a few months, at the most. I don't like being hindered by having to prescribe items for the person to buy there, thus, making more purchases, necessary or not. I once was in an argument when I refused to help a woman look for an ingredient for abortions. Sorry, that ain't me.

Botanicas are a staple of the spiritist culture and will always coexist alongside any of the houses of worship. Indeed, many go from these places of worship directly to the botanicas to stock up on supplies...Such is life...

TIDBITS, RECIPES, AND PRAYERS

In this chapter, I will provide certain insights that cropped up towards the end of this work. This book has taken longer than the first because of deteriorating eyesight. Being legally blind is quite frustrating for a writer like me who enjoys doing all of the physical work to bring this manuscript to life.

Karmic Love Over Centuries:

Over the years affinity has been studied and discussed more and more within spiritual circles. People who get along well and have many things in common possess this affinity. But affinity also makes its presence within reincarnation and karmic responsibilities and consequences.

Situations like the one I will be describing are common. Not constantly occurring, but often enough to leave a deep imprint in our daily lives. You enter a room or office and suddenly look up, as if programmed. And there they are…! You swear you've seen this person before. Indeed you **know** this person. Their thoughts, their inner soul, as well as the mirror that reflects back at you from his/her eyes.

All else in the room shifts to the background of your mind. Struggling to find a good reason to speak, you strike up a conversation that baits a response. It happens, and that is the beginning of an encounter with a soul mate. Someone who's been in your life before.

Before continuing further into the forest of affinity, there is one fact that all must understand. The nature of reincarnation involves lessons learned, lessons pending, justice baited, justice dealt upon. If a man, for example, was found guilty of domestic abuse towards his wife, the perfect justice would be that he be on the receiving end in the next life. As a consequence, his soul must leave the male body and culture, to be born again as a woman who will be abused by her husband, thereby providing the vessel of justice!

Correct, ladies and gentlemen, we incarnate as both sexes. Likewise, not everything involves the opposite gender. There is karma accumulated between all types of individuals. To name a few relationships that are ripe with karma stretching through reincarnation, there is parent to child, person to pet, criminal to victim. You get the idea. The Akashic Records at the spiritual board of Judgement, are filled to capacity.

In this era of evolvement the children are under the biggest pressure yet. The very existence of children is endangered as people abuse and kill more and more kids, causing the percentage of healthy offspring to dramatically drop. Although population throughout the planet will be growing, the quality of life will plummet. Pollution, garbage and recycling, as well as a water cycle that will handle the same drops as it has during all these centuries, will combine to provide very little peace and food. More mouths, the same amount of land and water, equal setting up for global warfare.

The great conflicts of tomorrow will emerge over water control and distribution, food rationing fairly, and infrastructure materials for building and maintaining the cities of tomorrow.

Where does this leave the mediums? What new course of spiritual action can we be expected to take? Will there be protection for spirit workers?

First of all, psychically gifted people will need to be focused on the purity of our drinking water as well as our agriculture. In these two areas of life accuracy will be a great asset. Parts of the globe will house water that perhaps you may not wish to drink. Halfway measures to insure quality of drinking water will cause great concern among the populace. Mediums will be called upon to team up with scientists to predict and find those areas of pure water. Likewise with agriculture. Mediums will be quite helpful in detecting good soil from that which is in decay.

This can bring about peaceful resolutions to problems of food and water, thus avoiding unnecessary conflicts between nations. Our skills will thrust us into the spotlight. This will bring about protection and inclusion.

One thing, though, about what this near future will look like. Necessity is the mother of invention. Governments will be forced to form spheres of influence and trade to distribute water and food fairly, therefore minimizing the suffering of conflicts over sustenance and survival. Whatever this entails as far as political.

Geography at the time, so be it. My spirits show me a time of great necessity to cooperate, whether it's dictatorships, democracies, theocracies, or parliamentary systems of rule. All prejudices and hatreds will have to be set aside when it comes to the very survival of the human race.

Of course, and sadly so, this will only happen after a period of disorder and war for control of areas rich in water and food. Places such as the Amazon rainforest, fertile farmlands, wetlands, and the Himalayas, to name a few ice-packed mountain ranges, will be targeted for control of these natural resources.

This time of tribulations will result in great strife, famine, and plagues. Radiation will factor in as part of the equation to solve the need for survival. All in all, the spirits foresee an intense, but short, period of pain. This will be followed by a new order of rule by fairness. Everyone will get some water and sustenance, perhaps not quite enough, but it will not be lopsided to the point that it triggers an endless cycle of conflicts. We must pray that our societal leaders exert common sense in order to be able to help humanity as a whole find a way out of this labyrinth of starvation.

Towards the end of the 21st Century, I predict these events will occur. They may be more or less as described above, but the essence of what my spirits see I will stand on. Remember, visions are never exact. The filter of our brain, with all of its accumulated views and prejudices, will always color our *evidencias*.

HOMAGE TO *LA SANTA MUERTE*

Many may know her as the Bone Mother, the Holy Death, la Nina Blanca, or Mother Reaper. Any way you call her, the Santa Muerte is an entity that stands all by herself, the sole ruler of her kingdom. She represents that which balances our birth. This balance of power provides a backdrop to the inevitable encounter of our soul with a return to the other side of the veil, which is our act of release from the prison of flesh.

In your local botanica you will find various images of her. She comes mainly in white or black. There are other colors available, but unless you know what they stand for with La Santa Muerte, stick to the basic white or black. There are many prayer and ritual books concerning devotion to her. Read carefully before you embark on petitioning an entity all too well known for swift and merciless justice. La Santa Muerte is a very jealous mother. Her devotees are quite careful not to offend her in any way, shape, or form. Likewise, they practice the Golden Rule to avoid being on the receptive end of justice.

My advice would be to begin with the white image. If you are a medium who is adept at lifting and combating evil, choose the black...or both, side by side. Look closely at the images in the botanica or supermarket where you wish to purchase her from. The image should communicate instant rapport with you. Place a finger gently on it. This should trigger the feeling of affinity even more so. Once you're satisfied that this particular image of La Santa Muerte is the one you want, bring her home.

Home is where you must be quite meticulous as to where to place her. She likes being a bit high, looking down on all who enter your home. If you have a temple in or outside of your home, you can also have her altar there. It all depends on what your Spirit Quadrant want you to do.

She MUST be alone, separate from all other images. Because of what she deals with, no other image can share her shelf or mini-altar. Even her candle or incense has to be away from the rest. The patroness of the Other Side deftly crosses the veil with instant dexterity.

Once she is located where you feel from her that she's comfortable, then you should have her offerings ready. The only beverage you can put in front of her, besides water, is genuine Tequila! No wine, run, firewater, or beer… Purely Tequila…! Flowers will vary according to your taste, or what you *feel* she wants from you. These can be all white or all dark colors, such as purple, maroon, or indigo. Cigarettes are preferred here, although little cigars will do.

Remember, she must be alone. There are but two exceptions. Photos or small images of the Virgin of Guadalupe, and St. Michael the Archangel. Our Lady of Guadalupe because she appeared in Mexico, where the cult to La Santa Muerte originated. St. Michael the Archangel represents God's commander-in-chief of Heaven's armies, a matter that is always of importance to La Santa Muerte.

In the beginning light white candles to her. Once you are more familiar—and careful—with her, you can study when to put a black candle or one of the other colors. Each color has a specific vibration for her, so read and study carefully to avoid costly mistakes.

One last comment on this. When embarking on your devotion to La Santa Muerte, please consult with someone who is already a devotee. If you can get hold of a Hispanic person, especially Mexican, even better. Just do not attempt this alone…! She is not for the faint of heart.

TIDBITS CONTINUED...

DRAGONS:

Creatures of intense emotions that are still a major part of the human experience. Beneficent harbingers of safety and health. Terrifyingly evil when venting their wrath! Heavenly to some, demons to others. Regardless of how they are viewed, dragons are an integral and permanent part of the spiritual world.

Beginning in East Asia, dragons are venerated as powerful angels, capable of saving human lives, granting wishes, and protecting shrines. There are three tiers of dragons. From lowest to highest, there's the three-toed creature, usually a sign of common society. Next is the five-toed dragon. This is representative of high social standing and greater power. The dragon with the seven toes, however, is reserved for the rulers, such as emperors, kings, and theocratic rulers.

They are worshipped as godly, and can be compared to the Western concept of archangels. Red is the predominant color. They can also be green, blue, and, the most sacred, a golden yellow. Many protective Oriental spirits camouflage as dragons, enabling them to avoid detection by the general public.

Moving West towards Europe, though, we come into conflicting winds of thought. Due to the combative nature of Christianity, with its aggressive, conquer and destroy all philosophy, dragons were made to occupy a different state of existence. It was ingrained into the European subconscious that dragons represented the devil and all evil in the world. Dragons were relegated to the same stage as serpents. These creatures exerted hypnotic power over people and caused them to commit acts of destruction on their fellow human. This was the teaching by the Christian priests and pastors early on. Indeed, many depictions of the saints show them defeating dragons, serpents, and sometimes winged creatures that represent the devil.

Yet, as luck would have it, not all legends of dragons were negative. Many were seen as vehicles for saviors. These were the minority, to be sure, but they did exist.

Me, I'll side with the Orient. I love my dragon spirits and have often dreamed of flying on one. When visiting Chinese New Year festivities I wait for the dragon to be paraded out. Tears of remembrance cloud my eyes, trophies from so many past incarnations in China as well as the rest of Asia. All my life since childhood I have yearned for all things Oriental. To this day, if I find myself in New York's or San Francisco's Chinatown, I'd better put a muzzle on my credit cards!!!

When only five years old, I would tell my mom, "I'm going to marry a Chinita…!" Well, the "Chinita" was in Puerto Rico. When I met my wife, everyone thought she was Chinese. She's one of the few in her family like that. Indeed, once in a Chinese restaurant they actually spoke Mandarin to her! They didn't quite know what to make of her…!

PRAYER AND SERVICE AGAINST EVIL:

Every once in a while, you may feel "off" your daily rhythm as your sense of order and cohesion in your life begins to hit road bumps. As events begin to add up, you begin wondering if you're under psychic attack or if you're being visited by one of the many stray souls causing havoc in people's lives.

Stray souls are those who, when in flesh, lived hard lives. They may have been orphans, homeless, abandoned, murdered, and forgotten upon crossing the veil. Most assuredly they never had prayers offered for the progress of their souls. Some were most probably used as pawns in negative witchcraft and are blindly searching for their victims.

Whichever path they led in physical life, they will surely continue in spirit life. Many a spirit of this persuasion has been lifted in mesas blancas (misas). However, one isn't always in a misa. So you are forced to put up a *servicio* or service to either send off, or hold out of the house.

There are many rituals for ridding your home or yourself from spirits that cause discomfort and upheaval. Be warned, though, that if things continue and grow out of hand a misa will definitely be in order. This is a generic example of a service to offer help and prayers for the errant soul to go on its way toward God.

For this service you will need the following:

Two household candles, white
Herbs such as rue, mint, basil, rosemary (either
in leaves or with stems)

A statue or stand-up picture of St. Michael the
Archangel
One goblet or wine glass that is almost full with
cold water from the faucet
Psalm 23

The first thing is to have a small table, stand, or appropriate
corner for the ritual. A white cloth will be the base. Onto
this cloth you will put the statue or image of St. Michael the
Archangel in the center. The two candles will be one on each
side of him. The goblet of water should be placed directly in
front of the Archangel, and, in front of that, a white plate with
the herbs on it.

Light the left candle first, then the right. The left symbolizes
the spiritual and the right the physical (material). The left is
always lit first. You then begin with the Lord's Prayer, the
Hail Mary, and Glory be to God. Next you freely speak and
invoke your Spirit Quadrant for assistance and blessings in the
traditional way you are used to.

Now you open the Bible to Psalm 23 and commence to
speak out loud. You will use words in a confident, commanding
voice. Instructing your Quadrant to call upon St. Michael the
Archangel for assistance in "escorting" whoever is the soul that
is disturbing the vibrational integrity of your home.

Picking up the herbs and holding them in a bunch, like a
duster, you then proceed from the back of the home to swat the
walls, or swipe the air, and do so following your instincts. Every
room in the house has to be done. Any screenporches, all closets,
bathrooms, and the garage have to be done. Pay special care to
the kitchen. The central axis of force in any home is the kitchen,

followed by the bathrooms. Ninety times out of one hundred it is in these two areas that negatives will settle in. Witchcraft that is sent into the home is usually focused on the kitchen and bathrooms for original access.

Once done the herbs are thrown out into an outside garbage can. The candles stay on until both extinguish. Leave this service in place three complete days. Say a closing prayer of your choice, then go on about your daily routine. You might want to light the candles and pray every day during the three days the service is standing. This will boost the energy being invoked.

CHISME BEAUTY...!

This word *chisme* [CHEES meh] means gossip. Holy molely! This is the one thing within the social mediumnistic circle that has caused more wars than humanity can count. . . Misas have been disrupted, sometimes violently, due to this indiscretion. Friendships and families have been split and rocked by gossip, not to speak of the endless mentoring bonds broken by this terrible habit within mediumnistic circles.

What on earth would people find to gossip about in this field? My dear reader, you would be surprised at the reasons for this "chisme" beauty. Beauty refers to the local hair salon or barber shop, where gossip gets **real** heavy. Yes, ladies, gentlemen can gossip more than the distaff side of the gender lawn.

Ego is usually a key player in this equation. Greed and envy also join the fray. To be fair, sometimes a genuine misunderstanding may also be the backdrop to a "they said, we said" drama.

If you speak to any psychologist or psychiatrist, they can attest to the Messiah Complex. These are individuals who see themselves as the only solution to another's problems. They take the good Samaritan action and stretch it until they practically rule the person they supposedly are helping. Instead of providing the help that any medium should, they hang on and literally run the client's life. You constantly hear of people who—pardon my words—won't sit on the toilet without asking permission from their spirit godmother or godfather...They submit their will power even in their love life. If the medium expresses displeasure with the choice of lover, it's only a matter of time before you see the break-up happening. Control over another is a two-way sword, for the controlling medium might have things backfire on them if the client feels all is not going perfectly well. The client will want to expiate their responsibilities onto the medium.

The result of all of this control and ego is often a rupture in relations. Playing with a client's path for your ego's sake, is not a safe position to be in. From these blowups the medium could expect their name to be dragged through the mud. These types of dependent souls are deadly in destroying a reputation. Even more so because this type of person will most assuredly hunt for another medium that will often be just as egotistic. As a result, the new medium will buy the client's sob story and send you negative vibes! And so the vicious cycle of ego continues. Beware of this situation...

Discernment is a necessary armament in this field. Mediums need to foment humility and honesty within the Great Work. Spiritism must be used as a tool to liberate individuals from evil and ill health, not a chain of dependency.

ONE-ON-ONE DEVELOPMENT

Methods of training developing mediums vary among spirit godparents. One of the best, but least used formula, involves one-on-one training. Many teach by having their trainees sit near them during misas. There are glaring differences between the two methods, but, when combined, they work well.

Having the developing medium sitting near or next to his/her mentor provides hands-on experience. They can observe the older mediums passing their quadrants as they, too, receive vibrations in the process. In a misa the presence of many spirit quadrants floods the atmosphere with vibrations that are felt throughout the ceremony. This can help the trainee spark their spirits awake. The presence of their godparent will be a cushion of safety in the event that intervention might be necessary. This could be necessary if the trainee is obviously a bit disorientated by the assault of vibrations, and the emotions that accompany them. It will boil down to on-the-job training which has its positive points.

I, however, have a marked preference for *beginning* the growth process with the one-on-one method. First, this gives the trainee and the mentor time for establishing a high degree of trust between them. The time for questions and answers provides even more basic preparation. Many of the skills to be learned by the new medium can be discussed at length.

One of the most important aspects to become familiar with will be what to do with those feelings of fear that come once the vibrations begin to jolt the spine and stand the hairs on end. The mentor must speak about what the medium will do when this begins. The medium must be told on how to properly help the spirit to, at least, pass and cleanse the aura. The technicalities in this field are numerous. The correct direction of fanning the back of the neck of the medium, the will power of the new medium to stay seated, and when to pass the spirit out into the surrounding space are critical lessons.

Teaching how to "read" the inspirations of the spirits is of paramount importance. The spirits will send thought patterns in the form of pictures and emotions. The interpretation by the medium is what determines their accuracy as a spiritist. Many tell me of their fear that they are imagining the images rather than actually receiving the message to be given to a client or to the congregation at a misa. All of these thoughts and actions take place in *seconds!*

Trust in themselves must be fomented by the mentor. As time evolves so must their trust in their spirits and, especially, in themselves. Over time they will learn to differentiate between their thoughts and those being transmitted to them from the other side of the veil of life. Imagine all of this in seconds: the physical passing of the spirit, the thoughts being analyzed, and the delivery—all in one split second!

But if you think that's rough, try training a new medium to give **voice** to a spirit. This will really test your patience, as it is the most complicated and challenging step in development. Remember, the process of using the medium's voice is just as new to the spirit as it is for the medium. In the beginning I teach my godkids to actually speak what they are being given in thought waves.

The very first step is teaching each spirit the proper greeting as they enter the medium's body. Usually the following statements are acceptable in a misa:

"May the peace of the Lord be here…"

"Peace and Justice…" The public answers, "Love and Charity."

"In God's name, I come in peace and love…"

This lays the groundwork for the sanctification of the arrival of a positive spirit at the misa. All will accept it as a spirit of goodness. Little by little the trainee will be able to hold onto the spirit for a longer time span, so that the entire message can be delivered or the work on the client can be finished properly. It will take a very long time for this process to settle in. Some take years, others take months. It all depends on the personality and character of the medium, as well as the type of Spirit Quadrant they are blessed with.

Guardian angels and the other angels that protect the medium could be of diverse origins. Many of these spirits may have known each other in other lives, and maybe not. A medium could have an African, a Viking, a courtesan, and a soldier in the same quadrant. The same applies to gender. The gender of the spirit will be reflected in what they had last incarnated. These spirits, though there is no real gender on the spirit side of life, will possess the gender identity of their last incarnation for identification purposes.

Culture, food preferences, even prejudices from this former life will come through. Over time, the medium must educate the spirits in prayer to elevate their existence and leave behind their past feelings. They must learn that they are sent here to help humanity, and, in so doing, are helping themselves to evolve to a higher plane.

Wrapping this up, the combination of both methods of training will provide the most successful path for any new medium. Begin with the one-on-one, and graduate to the hands-on. It will be a much more gentle transition.

THE GREAT OUTDOORS vs. THE PRIVATE INDOORS

Often I am asked if I can do a misa outdoors, either at the beach or in the woods. There are strict parameters that I impose on myself when it comes to misas in general. First, there must be privacy. Ample room is preferred. An easy to get to location is another parameter. And, of course, availability of bathrooms! Food can be brought either way.

I have held many misas outdoors in my lifetime. Most have been at the beach, my absolute favorite place to be. A good beach site is a bit easier to find than the woods. They are usually much more convenient to reach. The thing one must always look out for is the issue of privacy. It is best to look for a very quiet spot that is not frequented by many at all. Public beaches rarely are welcome areas for a misa. People and law enforcement may hinder your participation.

One of the few beaches I know of that openly allows the misas, the drummings, and the spirit dancing is Miami Beach, Florida. South Beach, famous for its free atmosphere and tolerance, usually is home to a Full Moon ceremony. Here, complete with African drums, dancing, musical instruments, and chanting, people celebrate the Moon in her many aspects. Diana, Nana-Buruku, Luna Madre and other titles attributed to the Moon are called on throughout the night. It should not be missed. Cameras are not welcome, unless you reach an agreement beforehand. South Beach is a place where privacy is the main currency!

Why not the back yard, you might ask? Easy answer... the neighbors. You can count on people gossiping and, worse yet, having some religious fanatic call the police to report a disturbance. The result will be a neighborhood problem. No thanks. It's bad enough when people see all those cars parked at your home and know that the "witching" has begun! Dear Lord, how humanity does lack the one thing it pretends to promote: *brotherhood and understanding!!!*

The religious fanaticism that characterizes so many religions is bringing the country and the world towards a major conflagration. For proof of this, if you are ever in Nuremberg, Germany, stop by the War Museum and see who issued the proclamation that Hitler was the Second Coming...

PUDDLES IN THE LIGHT

Scrying comes from the most rudimentary beginnings of humanity. Before there were mirrors, glass, or crystal balls, there was Nature. Oceans, lakes, rivers, waterfalls, pools, and underground sacred waters all provided the world's shamans with the tools for scrying and providing their flocks with futuristic readings and warnings, as well as healing.

The ability to read the images that bounce off the surface of a calm body of water have transferred down to the large goblet of water. The messages from the depths have also been assumed by the water receptacles. This doesn't mean that the natural waters have lost their use. Not at all. A medium that is skilled in scrying can use a puddle of water in mud the same way that they use a glass of water.

The sun or moon will emit rays that reveal the messages on these bodies of water. Periodically it's advisable to choose a spot outdoors and read the images that the water reveals. Alternate the practice using a differing body of water. Diversity will keep your "antenna" sharp.

Of all the bodies of water, perhaps the most popular are deep ponds or natural wells. More often than not their surface is smooth and dark to the naked eye. This enhances the ability to receive images and messages from the spirits. The next time you approach your boveda the confidence will color your interpretations, providing greater accuracy.

THE BOW AND ARROW

"My prayers are never answered! I pray and pray and pray until I'm blue in the face! Still—nothing…"

Boy, if I've heard the above a million times, it's been too little… Prayer has nothing to do with quantity. Five hundred repetitions of a particular prayer serve to hypnotize and provide emotional attachment to any religious situation. Likewise, the emotional rantings of loud, repetitive speakers. This mass hypnotism is used in many religious organizations today. It can submit your will to the speaker's objectives with ease, when you are sympathetic to his/her cause.

Indeed, I know witches that will lock themselves in a room and scream and pull their hair, or rip their clothes, just to persuade spirits and demons to perform the task they wish to achieve. Still others will spend hours on end meditating and visualizing a desired objective.

What they all don't realize is that one of the most direct paths of prayer is a lot less complicated than they are making it out to be. This brings me to the method I like to refer to as "The Bow and Arrow" prayer force. Bows and arrows are not exclusive to Indians of the Americas. Asia, Africa, and Europe have also extensive histories involving bows and arrows.

When you wish to pray for a desired goal, sit in a straight-backed chair that will keep your spine relatively upright. As you begin your prayer, asking for the desired goal, you are literally becoming the bow. With each passing word of your prayer the bow is drawn tighter and tighter. Once done communing with God and the powers that be, immediately turn away and immerse yourself in another activity that has absolutely nothing to do with your prayer.

This will then turn your thoughts from the prayer into the arrow as it flies off into the sea of spirituality. Your prayer will reach its intended target and will, in turn, be answered quicker. The more you dwell on what you prayed for, the longer it will hover over your head, anchored by you. Once you have entered another distinct activity unrelated to your prayer, the "arrow" is released. Thoughts have wings.

Remember to always add words that inform God and the powers that be of your acceptance of His will. It is always wise to acknowledge that our spirit quadrant and the Lord see much further out than we do. Things may not be as fruitful as you are sure they are. Looking out over time, our helpers may see that what you wish for in your prayer may turn into a disillusion. Always trust in God and add words that acknowledge that His will be done. If it's for you, all be it. If not, may He erase it from your mind.

Remember the method and thinking behind praying like a bow and arrow. Any good witch will tell you about this train of thought.

SAILING THE WATERS OF THE BOVEDA

We began in the boveda. We return to the boveda, sailing over the clear waters of our *cave*. Be still in your soul... Listen to the waters, as they whisper to your heart... The clarity of the glass, reflecting images and words from the surface, whispers to all of us. We must listen carefully. The naked eye will see nothing, much less anyone hear a sound. But those of us who have been gifted with the ability to use our physical five senses to decifer our sixth sense will know. We know that the boveda, or cave, is whispering secrets through the veil of life.

The simple waters of nature, resting in the goblet, protected from the outside world, talk to us. Wisdom, healing, battle, solutions, and a view of your path to growth, will flow from the boveda. The hidden cave, the secret trunk, the dark tunnel— the boveda—will release the secrets that have been waiting to be heard and acted upon.

Bless you all on your journey. While tackling the road of mediumnistic development, remember to stop by the caves of glass and liquid. Pause on your way and listen...

ABOUT THE AUTHOR

Florencio Guevara was born in New York City's borough of The Bronx, in 1946.

His parents were born in Puerto Rico. He has been happily married since 1977 and has two daughters and four grandchildren. He is legally blind, diabetes having claimed his peripheral vision. Besides his native New York, Florencio has lived in Puerto Rico, Miami, and is currently in Kissimmee. Soon, he will relocate to Port St. Lucie on Florida's Treasure Coast. Florida's Polk County area. Mr. Guevara is a retired teacher.

The author enjoys helping develop other mediums and spreading the seeds of the Great Work (La Obra). He has been a medium for over half a century, and considers it his life's work. His first book, <u>Mesa Blanca, the White Altar,</u> was many years in the works. Written specifically for the average person in as plain a language as possible, this sequel, <u>Whispers from the Cave,</u> will delve deeper into the technical workings of mediumship and spiritual recipes and prayers for specific needs of the soul. It will also explore the realities of life for mediums, from the battle against discrimination to the battles against in-house gossip and ego clashes. Development of mediumship is a never-ending classroom. There is no graduation… Until you are called through the Veil, you will be developing. Even then, another process of development will begin…

Lightning Source UK Ltd.
Milton Keynes UK
UKHW020628141222
413904UK00010B/1248